When Cam was done taking pictures, Mrs. Jansen gave her a sandwich and a drink.

"Please sit next to Eric," she said to Cam. "I'll take pictures, too."

Mrs. Jansen took a video camera from the canvas bag. "Smile," she told Cam and Eric. She took a video of them eating. Then she slowly turned and took a video of the tall buildings nearby and of people eating on the library steps.

"Help! Help!" a man yelled.

"Help!" he yelled again. "Help! A snake!"

CAM JANSEN

CASE #17

The Scary Snake
Mystery

David A. Adler
Illustrated by Susanna Natti

PUFFIN BOOKS
An Imprint of Penguin Group (USA) Inc.

PUFFIN BOOKS

Published by the Penguin Group

Penguin Young Readers Group, 345 Hudson Street, New York, New York 10014, U.S.A.

Penguin Group (Canada), 90 Eglinton Avenue East, Suite 700, Toronto, Ontario, Canada M4P 2Y3
(a division of Pearson Penguin Canada Inc.)

Penguin Books Ltd, 80 Strand, London WC2R 0RL, England

Penguin Ireland, 25 St Stephen's Green, Dublin 2, Ireland (a division of Penguin Books Ltd)

Penguin Group (Australia), 250 Camberwell Road, Camberwell, Victoria 3124, Australia
(a division of Pearson Australia Group Pty Ltd)

Penguin Books India Pvt Ltd, 11 Community Centre,
Panchsheel Park, New Delhi - 110 017, India

Penguin Group (NZ), 67 Apollo Drive, Rosedale, North Shore 0632, New Zealand
(a division of Pearson New Zealand Ltd)

Penguin Books (South Africa) (Pty) Ltd, 24 Sturdee Avenue,
Rosebank, Johannesburg 2196, South Africa

Registered Offices: Penguin Books Ltd, 80 Strand, London WC2R 0RL, England

First published in the United States of America by Viking,
a member of Penguin Putnam Inc., 1997

Published by Puffin Books, a division of Penguin Young Readers Group, 1999, 2005
This edition published by Puffin Books, a division of Penguin Young Readers Group, 2011

15 17 19 20 18 16 14

THE LIBRARY OF CONGRESS HAS CATALOGED THE VIKING EDITION AS FOLLOWS:
Adler, David A.
Cam Jansen and the scary snake mystery / David A. Adler ; illustrated by Susanna Natti.
p. cm.—(A Cam Jansen adventure ; 17)
Summary: Cam investigates when a thief steals her mother's video camera
and a tape containing footage of a big scary snake.
ISBN: 0-670-87517-1 (hardcover)
[1. Mystery and detective stories.]
I. Natti, Susanna, ill. II. Title. III. Series: Adler, David A. Cam Jansen adventure ; 17.
PZ7.A2615Caq 1997
[Fic]—dc21
97-2627 CIP AC

Puffin Books ISBN 978-0-14-240288-7

Printed in the United States of America

RL: 2.3

To great fans of Cam Jansen,
Adam
Joshua
Sammy
Jason
and Rachel

Chapter One

"Coming through! Coming through!" a man pushing a long rack of clothing called out.

Mrs. Jansen took her daughter Cam's hand and pulled her out of the man's way.

"Watch out!" a woman in a brown uniform coming from the other direction said. She was pushing a cart loaded with packages. This time it was Cam's friend Eric Shelton who was in the way. He quickly stepped aside.

The sidewalk and crosswalks were crowded

with people rushing about. More people kept coming out of the large office buildings.

"I love the city," Eric said. "It's so busy and exciting here. Maybe we'll see a movie star or an author or a baseball player."

"Mom brought along a video camera," Cam told Eric. "If we see someone famous, she can take a movie of him. We can send it to the 'News Scoop' contest and maybe win a prize."

A young man eating an ice cream cone bumped into Cam. Some ice cream dripped onto her shirt.

"I'm sorry," he called as he hurried off.

Mrs. Jansen gave Cam a tissue. Cam wiped the ice cream off her shirt and asked, "What's the rush? Where is everyone going?"

"This is a busy section of the city," Mrs. Jansen explained. "People are making deliveries. It's lunchtime, too. Some people are probably hungry and in a rush to eat."

"I am!" Cam said. "I'm hungry and in a rush to eat."

"We'll eat as soon as we find a place to sit. I brought sandwiches and drinks," Mrs. Jansen said. "Then we'll go to the art museum."

It was the last day of summer vacation. Cam, Eric, and Mrs. Jansen were in the city to see an exhibit of paintings by Henri Matisse.

They walked a few more blocks until they came to a large library. People were seated on the wide steps leading to the entrance of the library. Some were eating. Some were reading. One man sitting on the bottom step was feeding bread crumbs to pigeons.

"Let's sit here," Mrs. Jansen said.

Eric and Mrs. Jansen sat on one end of the steps, close to one of two large stone lions. Mrs. Jansen took a sandwich and a juice container from the yellow canvas bag she was carrying. She gave them to Eric. She took another sandwich and drink and offered them to Cam.

"Not now, Mom. I'll eat, but first I want to take a picture of the lions. I want to remember them."

Cam looked straight at the lions. She blinked her eyes and said, *"Click."* She looked at her mother and Eric. She blinked her eyes and said, *"Click"* again.

Cam wasn't taking pictures with a real camera. She was using her *mental camera,* her memory.

Cam Jansen has an amazing photographic memory. It seems to Cam that she has a camera in her head and photographs of whatever she has seen. Cam blinks her eyes and says, *"Click"* whenever she wants to remember something. Cam says "*Click*" is the sound her mental camera makes when it takes a picture.

Cam's real name is Jennifer Jansen. When she was just a baby, some people called her "Red," because she has bright red hair. But when they found out about her amazing memory they began calling her "The Camera." Soon "The Camera" was shortened to "Cam."

When Cam was done taking pictures, Mrs. Jansen gave her a sandwich and a drink.

"Please sit next to Eric," she said to Cam. "I'll take pictures, too."

Mrs. Jansen took a video camera from the

canvas bag. "Smile," she told Cam and Eric. She took a video of them eating. Then she slowly turned and took a video of the tall buildings nearby and of people eating on the library steps.

"Help! Help!" a man yelled.

"Help!" he yelled again. "Help! A snake!"

Chapter Two

Cam and Eric turned to look at the man. Mrs. Jansen turned, too. Many people gathered near the cement lions to see what was happening.

The man threw his sandwich to the sidewalk. He jumped up and moved to a higher step.

Near him was a young woman with long blond hair. At her feet was a large burlap bag. A snake had crawled out of the bag.

Hiss!

The snake looked around. Its forked tongue darted out of its mouth.

Hiss!

It turned toward two old women who were walking by.

"Help! Help! I'm afraid of snakes," one of the women yelled.

"Well, I'm not," the other woman said. Then she put her hands on her hips, leaned forward, and said to the snake, "Hiss, hiss yourself."

The young woman grabbed the snake. She

put it into the burlap bag and held the bag closed.

The man walked over and pointed to a sandwich on the sidewalk and shouted, "That snake bit my cream cheese sandwich!"

"I'm sorry," the young woman said. "But I'm sure Scaly didn't bite your sandwich. He doesn't eat bread or cream cheese. He only eats live mice."

"Yuck!" someone in the crowd said.

"Live mice!" someone else said. "That's disgusting!"

The man looked at his sandwich. It was on the sidewalk, and two pigeons were pecking at it.

"Here," the young woman said. She gave the man some money. "I'm sorry. Why don't you buy something else to eat."

The man took the money.

"I'm not afraid of most animals," the man said as he walked toward a hot dog and soda wagon, "but that's a scary snake."

People who had gathered to watch started to walk away.

"Wow!" Eric said. "That's why I love being in the city. You can see just about anything here."

"Hey, Mom," Cam said. "The red light of your camera is still on. You're still filming."

Mrs. Jansen pressed a button. The red light went off.

"Before the man screamed, I was looking at you through the camera and filming. When he yelled 'Help!' I turned and looked through the camera at him and the snake."

Mrs. Jansen put the camera back in the yellow canvas bag. She sat with Cam and Eric. While they ate lunch, Eric kept watching the young woman and the burlap bag.

Eric said, "Maybe Scaly will sneak out again."

Scaly didn't.

Cam, Eric, and Mrs. Jansen finished eating. Then Cam threw the sandwich wrappers and the empty juice containers in the nearby trash basket. Mrs. Jansen put the canvas bag on her shoulder.

"Now, let's go to the museum," she said.

"I love museums," Eric said as they got up. "At the Kurt Daub Museum, I saw an old airplane and dinosaur skeletons."

"That's a science museum. We're going to an art museum," Mrs. Jansen explained.

"I like art, too," Eric said.

They walked down a few steps to the sidewalk. Someone wearing sunglasses, a blue hooded sweatshirt, and jeans walked down, too.

Cam, Eric, and Mrs. Jansen walked to the corner. The person in the blue sweatshirt was right behind them.

Eric whispered, "I think we're being followed."

Cam turned to look at the man. His face was hidden behind his sunglasses and inside the hood of his sweatshirt.

The traffic light was red. The DON'T WALK sign was on. Cam, Eric, and Mrs. Jansen stopped at the corner and waited for the light and sign to change.

The man in the sweatshirt grabbed the canvas bag off Mrs. Jansen's shoulder. He ran across the street, still holding the bag.

"Help! Help! I've been robbed!" Mrs. Jansen shouted.

Chapter Three

Mrs. Jansen stepped into the street to follow the thief.

Honk!

She quickly stopped. The light was still red. The sign still said DON'T WALK, and cars were speeding by.

Honk! Honk! Honk!

The thief was almost hit by a taxi cab. The cab stopped. The window was open and the driver waved his fist at the thief.

Cam looked at the thief as he ran across

the street. She blinked her eyes and said,
"Click."

"Help!" Mrs. Jansen said again. "I've been
robbed."

"We can't help you until the traffic light
changes," a woman told Mrs. Jansen. "It's too
dangerous to cross against the light."

"By then," a man said, "the thief will probably be far away."

"Stop that thief!" Mrs. Jansen yelled to the people across the street. But they didn't seem to hear her.

Cam, Eric, and Mrs. Jansen watched the thief turn at the corner across the street. He ran down Fourth Avenue. Cam blinked her eyes again and said, *"Click."*

The traffic light changed to green. The sign said WALK.

Cam, Eric, and Mrs. Jansen hurried across the street. Then Cam and Eric ran ahead.

"Be careful," Mrs. Jansen called as she tried to keep up with them.

Cam and Eric ran together down Fourth Avenue. Ahead of them was a short man carrying several large packages.

Cam ran to the left of the man. Eric ran to the right. The man moved to get out of Cam's way and Eric ran right into him. Packages fell onto Eric and the sidewalk.

"I'm sorry. I'm sorry," Eric said.

Eric quickly picked up some of the packages and gave them to the man. Then he picked up the other packages and tried to give them to the man, too.

"Not so fast! Not so fast!" the man said as he tried to hold onto everything.

Mrs. Jansen took Eric's hand.

"I'm glad I have you. Where's Cam?"

"She ran ahead," Eric told her. "She's trying to catch the thief."

The short man was still struggling with the packages. Two were still on the sidewalk.

Mrs. Jansen smiled and said, "Let me help."

She tucked one package under each of his arms.

"I'm really sorry Eric bumped into you," she told the man. "I was just robbed, and he was in a hurry to follow the thief."

"That's too bad," the man said. "Last week I thought someone stole my eyeglasses, but then I found them under a chair."

"Someone in a blue sweatshirt pulled my camera bag off my shoulder and ran off with it."

"Oh, my," the man said. "You really were robbed. I hope you catch the thief."

Mrs. Jansen held onto Eric's hand and walked quickly with him to the next corner. Cam was standing there, waiting for the traffic light to change. Mrs. Jansen took Cam's hand.

"Don't run away from me again," Mrs. Jansen said. "You could get lost."

Cam said, "I think I saw him way ahead, but I can't be sure."

Eric told Cam, "Say *'Click.'* Look at the picture you have stored in your head. Then you'll know if he is the thief."

"I said *'Click,'* but with the sunglasses and the hood, I never really got a good look at him. That's why I'm not sure."

"We shouldn't chase after him," Mrs. Jansen said to the children. "He could be dangerous. Let's go to the museum. When we get there, I'll phone the police. They'll tell us what to do."

Mrs. Jansen held firmly onto Cam and Eric's hands. They walked across the street.

"Look," Cam whispered. She pointed to someone leaving a building. He wasn't wearing sunglasses. But he was wearing a blue

sweatshirt and jeans. He was just a short distance ahead of them.

Cam blinked her eyes and whispered, *"Click."*

The man quickly turned and went the other way.

"That sweatshirt has a hood," Eric whispered. "I think he's the thief!"

Chapter Four

Cam closed her eyes and said, *"Click."* She said, *"Click"* again.

Cam opened her eyes. "I'm sure that's him. There's an ink spot on his pants, right near his left pocket. I saw a spot just like that on the thief's pants. Let's go after him."

"We won't chase him," Mrs. Jansen said. "We'll follow him. And we won't get too close. He might be dangerous."

Cam and Eric walked ahead. When they got to the corner, they stopped.

"There he is," Cam said, and pointed.

The man had turned the corner and was walking down Broadway. Cam looked back, smiled, and waved so her mother would know where they were going. Then Cam and Eric followed the man.

The man was walking quickly. He turned and saw Cam and Eric. Then he started to run. He bumped into some people as he ran, but he didn't stop. At the corner, the man quickly crossed the street.

"Wait! Wait for me," Mrs. Jansen called. She caught up with Cam and Eric just as they were about to cross the street.

The man in the sweatshirt ran straight down the next block. There were two police officers standing at the corner.

"Stop! Stop that thief!" Cam called. She pointed to the man in the blue sweatshirt. One of the officers stopped him.

"Hey, what did I do?" the man asked.

Cam, Eric, and Mrs. Jansen caught up to

him. He had brown curly hair and freckles across his nose.

"Why were you running?" one of the police officers asked the man.

"Why was *I* running? These people were chasing me. That's why I was running. And anyway, I'm in a hurry to get someplace."

Cam said, "He's running because he stole

my mother's camera. That's why he's running. He's a thief."

"Was something stolen?" one of the officers asked Mrs. Jansen.

"My camera was taken," Mrs. Jansen said. "It was in a large canvas bag. Someone pulled it right off my arm."

"A camera? Was it one of those small pocket cameras?" the man asked.

Cam pointed at the man and said, "You know what it was. It was a video camera. And you took it!"

The man smiled. "And where did I put it?" he asked. "I don't have any camera and I don't have any yellow bag."

The man wasn't carrying anything. He was wearing a sweatshirt, jeans, and sneakers. There were two large openings in the front of his sweatshirt. It was a place for him to keep his hands warm on cold days. There was no place for him to hide a large canvas bag and camera.

"You're right," Mrs. Jansen said softly. "You don't have my camera. I'm sorry."

"I'm sorry we stopped you," one of the police officers told the man. "You can go now, but don't run."

The man turned and walked away quickly.

One of the officers said to Mrs. Jansen, "If your camera was stolen, you should go to the police station. An officer there can fill out a report."

The police station was just two blocks away.

Mrs. Jansen took Cam and Eric's hands. "Thank you for your help," she said to the police.

Chapter Five

"That was just terrible," Mrs. Jansen told Cam and Eric as they walked away. "You accused an innocent man of being a thief."

"But he *is* a thief," Cam said. "I looked at the pictures I have in my head. That was the same sweatshirt. Those were the same jeans with the same ink spot near the left pocket."

"He didn't have the camera," Mrs. Jansen said, "so he wasn't the thief."

"But, Mom!"

"I don't want to hear any more about it. We're going to the police station. Then we can go to the museum."

At the police station, Mrs. Jansen told Cam and Eric to sit on one of the benches. She went to the front desk. The officer there asked her some questions and he filled out a report.

When she was done, she told Cam and Eric, "We're going to the museum now. Don't run ahead and don't chase after people. Stay with me."

Cam, Eric, and Mrs. Jansen walked down Lincoln Avenue. "I'm not going to let a stolen camera ruin our day," Mrs. Jansen said. "It's gone and that's it."

Mrs. Jansen walked slowly. She stopped often to show Cam and Eric important buildings and to look in store windows.

Mrs. Jansen told the children what they would see at the museum. "Henri Matisse painted in bright, bold colors. You'll love his work."

They reached Fourth Avenue and turned.

Cam told Eric, "This is where I first saw the man again."

They came to a store with big signs taped in the windows.

CLOSED.

OUT OF BUSINESS.

Cam said, "The man was coming out of this store."

The store had two large front windows. Be-

tween the windows was an entranceway that led to the door. Cam, Eric, and Mrs. Jansen looked through the first window. No one was in there, just boxes and lots of papers on the floor.

Cam's mother said, "He couldn't have been in here. The store is closed."

"Maybe this is where he met his 'fence,'" Cam said.

Mrs. Jansen looked in the window. "There are no fences in there, and no gates, either."

"Oh, Mom," Cam said. "A 'fence' is someone who buys stolen things from thieves and sells them to other people."

"Well," Mrs. Jansen said. "He's not in there. The store is empty."

They walked past the entrance.

"Look!" Cam said, pointing. "There it is!"

On the floor by the front door was a large yellow canvas bag.

Chapter Six

Mrs. Jansen ran to the bag and opened it.

"It's my bag," she said. "My camera is still in it."

Mrs. Jansen picked up the bag. "I'm so glad you found this," she said.

Cam looked in the canvas bag. Then she looked into the store entranceway. "This is a real mystery," she said.

"There's no mystery," her mother told her. "I have my camera back."

"But why did the thief steal it and then leave it here?" Cam asked.

"This is an old video camera," Mrs. Jansen answered as they walked. "Maybe he wanted a newer model."

Eric said, "Maybe he was afraid he would get caught."

"We *did* catch him," Cam said. "But because he no longer had the camera, the police let him go."

Mrs. Jansen said, "They were right to let him go. He isn't really a thief. Since I have my camera back, he didn't really *steal* it. He just *borrowed* my camera."

Mrs. Jansen held the yellow bag very close as they walked along Fourth Avenue to the museum.

"I remember something you said," Eric told Cam's mother as they walked, "and it proves that Cam stopped the real thief. You told the police your camera was in a large canvas bag."

"It is," Mrs. Jansen said.

Eric went on. "But the thief said, 'I don't have any camera and I don't have any *yellow* bag.' How did he know the bag is yellow?"

"You're right," Cam said. "He could only have known the bag is yellow if he took it."

"And *you're* right, too," Eric said. "He was the thief."

Mrs. Jansen said, "And now *I'm* right. If nothing was stolen, there was no thief."

There was a long line of people waiting to see the Matisse exhibit. Mrs. Jansen checked the canvas bag in the coatroom. Then Cam, Eric, and Mrs. Jansen went to the end of the line.

While they waited, Mrs. Jansen pointed to a large poster. It had a shape that looked like a wolf's head against a bright purple, blue, green, and orange background. Under it were the dates of the Matisse exhibit.

"Isn't that beautiful?" Mrs. Jansen asked.

"It's very nice," Cam said. But she wasn't really looking at the poster. She was still thinking about the "borrowed" camera.

When they entered the exhibit hall, Mrs. Jansen pointed to one of the paintings. "Isn't that beautiful?" she asked.

"It's very nice," Cam said.

Eric said, "I think this picture is a little scary. Those shapes look like lizards."

Cam whispered to Eric, "We know who took the camera, but we don't know why."

Eric whispered back, "Your mother is right. Nothing was really stolen. Let's just forget it."

They all walked to another room in the museum.

Mrs. Jansen pointed to another painting.

"These shapes are beautiful, not scary," Eric said.

"It's very nice," Cam said, without even looking at the painting. She was still thinking about the camera.

Mrs. Jansen stopped in front of the paintings and looked carefully at each one.

Eric looked, too. He told Cam he especially liked one of the paintings. Without looking, Cam said again, "It's very nice."

On their way to the next room, they passed through a wide hall. There were water fountains, public telephones, and framed posters in the hall.

"Oh, my. Look at that picture," Eric said. He pointed to a poster. "It should be called, 'Dragons, Lizards, and a Horse.'"

"Look over there," Mrs. Jansen said, and pointed. She was pointing to a blank white wall. "I think it's the nicest painting in the exhibit. What do you think?" she asked Cam.

"It's very nice."

Eric and Mrs. Jansen laughed.

"What's so funny?" Cam asked. "I said it's very nice."

Cam's mother told her to look at what she said was very nice.

Cam looked up. She stared at the wall. Then she said very slowly, "There's no picture."

"It was a joke," her mother told her.

"There's no picture," Cam said again.

"Now look over here at a picture I like," Eric said, and pointed to the left. "Do you see all the dragons?"

This time Cam did look. She pointed to a long, curved yellow line that ran across the picture. "And that looks like a yellow snake," Cam said slowly.

Cam looked away from the wall.

"There's no picture and there's a snake picture," Cam said. "There's no picture and there's a snake picture," she said again, and closed her eyes.

Cam was thinking.

Mrs. Jansen and Eric stood by Cam and waited.

"No picture and a snake picture," Cam said to herself. Then she opened her eyes and looked at her mother and Eric. "That blank wall and the snake picture gave me the answer. I think I solved the mystery."

Chapter Seven

"Do you know why the thief took the camera and then left it in that doorway?" Eric asked. "Did he change his mind? Did he know we were following him? Did he get scared?"

"He didn't change his mind," Cam said, "and he wasn't scared."

"Then what happened?" Eric asked.

"Before I tell you," Cam said, "we have to get the camera back. I have to see if I'm right."

Mrs. Jansen said, "We'd have to go to the

coatroom to get the camera, and there are still some paintings we haven't seen."

"Please, Mom."

"Can't you just tell us what you think happened?" Mrs. Jansen asked Cam.

Cam shook her head. "I want to be sure I'm right."

"Oh, my," Mrs. Jansen said. "We came here to see beautiful art, not to solve mysteries. But I do want to know why he took the camera and left it."

Mrs. Jansen thought for a moment. Then

she said, "We'll walk quickly through the rest of the show. Then I'll get my camera and you can tell us why that man borrowed it."

Mrs. Jansen quickly led Cam and Eric to the next room.

Cam looked at a painting and said, "Henri Matisse was a great artist. I like looking at his paintings. I just like solving mysteries more."

Mrs. Jansen stopped for a moment in the last room. She smiled and said, "I could just stay here forever."

"I hope she isn't serious," Cam whispered to Eric.

"I heard that," Mrs. Jansen said. "And we can go now."

Mrs. Jansen gave the man in the coatroom her claim ticket. He gave her the yellow canvas bag.

Cam told her mother, "Now take a movie of me."

"Not in here," Mrs. Jansen said. "It's too dark. I'll do it outside."

They went to the sculpture garden. Mrs. Jansen took the camera out of the yellow bag. "Smile," she said as she looked through the camera and pressed a button.

Mrs. Jansen pressed the button again.

"Hey," she said. "It doesn't work."

Eric said, "The thief broke the camera!"

"No, he didn't," Cam said. "If you open it, you'll know what he stole."

Mrs. Jansen pressed a button. The side of the camera popped open.

"The video tape is gone," Mrs. Jansen said. "He stole the tape!"

"He can film over it," Eric said. "He'll use it in his own camera."

"I have such wonderful things on that tape," Mrs. Jansen said. "I have pictures of Dad's surprise birthday party and of both of you swimming in the lake."

"The Matisse snake pictures gave me the answer," Cam said. "You looked at Scaly through the camera when it was still running. You took a video of Scaly scaring that man."

Mrs. Jansen asked, "Why would he want pictures of a snake?"

"He's planning to sell it," Cam explained. "He wants to win the 'News Scoop' contest. The local TV station will pay a lot of money for any film they use."

Eric said, "The thief heard Cam when she

said that the red light was still on. That's why he followed us and took the camera."

"He got rid of the camera because he was afraid he might get caught," Cam explained. "And he *did* get caught. But without the camera, the police let him go."

"If there's a prize for that tape," Mrs. Jansen said, "we should get it and not some thief. I would also love to get back the pictures of Dad's surprise party and of you at the lake."

Mrs. Jansen went into the museum again. In the front lobby were public telephones and a large telephone book. She looked through the book.

"Here's the number of the local television station," she said. "Cam, please keep your finger right here." Mrs. Jansen took a handful of coins from her purse. She looked at the number Cam was pointing to and dialed the telephone.

"Hello. . . . Yes, I'll wait."

Mrs. Jansen waited.

"Hello. . . . Yes, I'm still waiting."

Mrs. Jansen waited some more. Then she said, "I want to speak with someone about the 'News Scoop' contest. . . . Yes, I'll wait."

She waited again.

Mrs. Jansen finally had a chance to explain what had happened to the tape. Then she listened for a while. She said, "Thank you," and hung up the telephone.

"She didn't help me," Mrs. Jansen told Cam and Eric. "She said she didn't see any snake tape. And whatever tapes they do have belong to the television station."

Mrs. Jansen looked at Cam and Eric. "I may not have the tape," she said, "and we may not get the prize money. But I still have Dad and you, and that's more important. I'll just buy a new tape and take new movies."

Chapter Eight

Eric went home with Cam and her mother. Before dinner, Cam and Eric sat on the floor of the living room and played a board game. Mr. and Mrs. Jansen watched the news on television.

"Today was a beautiful day," the newscaster said near the end of the program. "It was sunny and warm. It was a great day to take your pet outside. Let's look at someone who took her pet outside and someone who wasn't very happy about it. It's today's 'News Scoop' winner!"

Cam and Eric looked up.

A newswoman in a red jacket was smiling. Then on the TV screen was a picture of Scaly. His tongue darted out toward the man's sandwich.

"That's my tape," Mrs. Jansen said. "It won today's 'News Scoop' contest. I'm going right to the television station and tell them that I took that video."

"I don't think they'll give you back your tape," Mr. Jansen said, "but if you're going to the television station, I'll go with you."

"Then Eric and I have to go, too," Cam said. "We're too young to stay home alone."

In the car, Mrs. Jansen said she deserved the "News Scoop" prize. Mr. Jansen said he didn't think she would get the prize money.

At the television station, Mrs. Jansen told the man sitting behind the front desk, "You showed my tape tonight. I'm tonight's 'News Scoop' winner."

"Then you'll get a check for the prize money in the mail," the man said.

"Oh, no, you don't understand," Mrs. Jansen said. She began to tell him all about the stolen camera and the museum and Cam's photographic memory.

The man waved his hand. He asked Mrs. Jansen to stop and please sit down. Then he picked up a telephone and asked for someone to come to the lobby.

Cam, Eric, and Cam's parents sat on a long couch and waited. Then a woman in a red jacket came out. She was the newswoman they had seen on TV.

She smiled. "Hello. My name is Penny Kelly. Please follow me to my office."

Cam, Eric, and Cam's parents walked with Penny Kelly past a large window next to a closed door. On the other side of the window was a studio. Above the door was a sign, QUIET—ON THE AIR. Penny Kelly led them to a small office. The desk was covered with papers.

"You said the snake tape is yours," Penny Kelly said. "It's not. It's ours. We bought it this afternoon from a young man."

"He didn't take that video," Mrs. Jansen said. "I did."

Cam closed her eyes and said, *"Click."* Then, with her eyes still closed, she asked, "Was the young man wearing jeans and a blue sweatshirt? Does he have brown curly hair, brown eyes, and about twenty freckles on his

nose? Was there an ink stain near the left pocket of his jeans?"

"I didn't count his freckles and I didn't check if his jeans were clean," Penny Kelly said. "But everything else sounds right."

"He's a thief!" Mrs. Jansen told Penny Kelly. "He stole that tape."

"I'm sorry, but he came here and sold it to us. Unless you can prove it's yours, there's nothing I can do."

Mrs. Jansen frowned. "I can't prove it's mine," she said. "It just is."

"I'm sorry," Penny Kelly said again.

She led everyone out of her office. They walked through the hall, toward the exit. They were right outside the studio when Cam's father said, "I'm not surprised. I didn't think they would give you the prize."

"You're not surprised!" Cam said. "Surprised! That's it! I can prove it's our tape!"

Penny Kelly pointed to the QUIET—ON THE AIR sign. "How can you prove it?" she whispered.

"Earlier on the tape," Cam said, "are pictures of us shouting, 'Surprise!'"

"It was at a party for my birthday," Mr. Jansen whispered.

"Just rewind the tape," Cam told Penny Kelly. You'll see it's ours."

They all went back to the office. Penny Kelly took a tape off her desk. She put it in the VCR and pressed the rewind button. She turned on the TV behind her desk and pressed the play button. On the screen was a picture of a large platter of small sandwiches.

"That's the party and those are egg-salad sandwiches," Mrs. Jansen said. "They were delicious."

"Surprise!" people shouted. There was a picture of a very surprised Mr. Jansen.

"This *is* your tape," Penny Kelly said. She took it out of the machine and gave it to Mrs. Jansen.

"It's too bad the thief got away," Mr. Jansen said. "He got our 'News Scoop' prize money."

"No, he didn't," Penny Kelly said.

She took a book off her desk. "I have his name and address right here. We were going to send him a check to pay for the tape. Now, I'll give his name to the security office. They may have him arrested."

Mrs. Jansen looked at the name. Next to it was a number.

"Wow! Is that how much you were going to pay him?"

Penny Kelly said, "Yes. Now we'll send the

check to you." Mrs. Jansen wrote their address in the book.

Cam's mother shook Penny Kelly's hand and thanked her.

Mr. Jansen thanked her, too.

Mrs. Jansen said, "Let's go home now. I'm hungry."

"I'm too tired to cook," Mr. Jansen said. Then he smiled. "You just won the 'News Scoop' prize, so let's all go to a restaurant and celebrate."

"A restaurant," Mrs. Jansen said. She smiled, too.

Cam looked at her smiling parents. She blinked her eyes and said, *"Click."*